Titanic
Death on the Water

For Sally/Mum,
who had to put up with all the complaining

First published 2012 by
A & C Black, an imprint of Bloomsbury Publishing plc
50 Bedford Square, London WC1B 3DP

www.acblack.com

ISBN 978-1-4081-5581-3

A CIP catalogue for this book is available from the British Library.

Printed by CPI Group (UK), Croydon, CR0 4YY

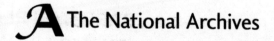 The National Archives

TITANIC

Death on the Water

Tom & Tony Bradman

A & C Black • London

A The National Archives

The National Archives is the UK government's official archive, containing over a thousand years of history. They give detailed guidance to government departments and the public sector on information management and advise others about the care of historical archives.

www.nationalarchives.gov.uk

Contents

Chapter One

A Well-Respected Man

It was a terrible thing to admit even to himself, but Billy was glad his Da was dead.

Maybe *glad* was a bit strong, he thought as he looked down at the coffin in the open grave; *relieved* would be a better word. He was definitely relieved.

Billy glanced guiltily at Ma. She was standing beside him in the circle of mourners and stared straight ahead, her eyes dry, although her face was pale and drawn from all the crying she had done over the last week. Beyond her, Billy's sisters sobbed uncontrollably. Ada, Nelly, Daisy and little six-year-old Mabel were dark-haired and brown-eyed like Da, and pretty too, while

Billy had Ma's sandy looks and blue eyes. But Billy was tall like his Da.

It was a bitterly cold March day in Belfast and a sharp wind brought the salt tang of the Irish Sea into the graveyard. Ma gripped Billy's hand. The Reverend Magill – vicar of Trinity, their local church – was coming to the end of the service. 'Therefore O Lord, we commit thy servant's body to the ground,' he droned. 'Earth to earth, ashes to ashes, dust to dust, in sure and certain hope of resurrection to eternal life, through our Lord Jesus Christ...'

Then it was over. A couple of men began shovelling dark soil into the grave and the crowd of black-clad mourners moved away. The Reverend came up to shake Ma's hand. 'A fine turn-out today, Mrs Fleming,' he said. 'But that's no surprise. Your Robert was always a well respected man.'

'Aye, so he was,' said Ma. She looked at Billy and he quickly lowered his gaze. Sometimes he felt she could see right inside his mind. 'You'll be coming back to the house for some tea and cake, Reverend?' she went on.

'Of course,' said the Reverend. 'It's kind of you to ask.'

Ma, Billy and the girls went home in the undertaker's carriage that had brought them. Mabel stopped crying, so fascinated was she by the horses, a pair of coal-black stallions with black feather head-dresses.

Billy stared out at the terraces of red-brick houses. His Da had been a well respected man right enough, but he had also been a difficult man to live with. Especially if you were his son and didn't want to follow the path he had chosen for you.

Da had been a fitter at the Harland and Wolff shipyard, a skilled man, and he'd said it was the best job in Belfast. He'd started as a fourteen-year-old apprentice and couldn't understand why Billy didn't jump at the chance to do the same. They had argued, and Ma had tried to make peace between them, but there could only have been one end to their quarrel.

Two months ago, on the day he'd turned fourteen, Billy had left school and started at the shipyard.

Ma had laid the table in the parlour before they had left for the funeral. As soon as they were indoors she uncovered the cakes and sandwiches.

'Will I be pouring the tea, Ma?' said Billy, keen to help.

'You most certainly will not,' said Ma, giving him a stern look. 'You're the man of the house now, Billy. Your job is to welcome our guests.'

Someone was already knocking at the door, and for the next half hour Billy was kept busy ushering people in until the small house was packed. There were aunts and uncles and cousins galore, friends of the family and Da's workmates and plenty of people Billy didn't know from Adam. They all murmured their condolences to Ma then stood talking to each other in hushed voices.

Da's workmates stayed in the hall and ended up sitting on the stairs. They reminded Billy of a picture he'd seen at Sunday school, a line of angels ascending to heaven. But Da's workmates were no angels, they were hard like Da. How could they be anything else? Working in the shipyard was dangerous and they risked their lives every day. Da had been hammering rivets fifty feet up the side of a hull when the plank he was standing on had given way.

'Have you not got anything a wee bit stronger, Billy?' said one of the men. It was strange to see them in their Sunday best and not their caps and working clothes and heavy boots. It was even stranger not to hear them continually swearing and cursing and taking the Lord's name in vain. 'We can't give your Da a proper send-off with nothing to drink but tea. Did he not keep a bottle hidden from your Ma somewhere? Find it for us, there's a good lad.'

'I'll see what I can do,' said Billy, and headed for the scullery. He was used to being given orders. For the last two months Da and his workmates had sent him on errands all over the shipyard, many of them practical jokes. Not that he'd minded being told to ask at the stores for a left-handed bolt wrench or a packet of sky-hooks, even though such things didn't exist. He had been more worried by the fact that every-thing in the shipyard terrified him.

Da had sometimes taken him to the shipyard when he was younger and it had always reminded him of other pictures he'd seen at Sunday school – those of Hell. The shipyard was a place of sound and fury and constant movement, of sudden showers of sparks and clanging steel and men having to do ridiculously dangerous things as a normal part of their jobs.

Da and his workmates made light of it and told black jokes about men being crushed unexpectedly or mistakenly sealed into tiny compartments at the bottom of hulls. Billy had listened, taking it all in, and a small, frightened voice inside him had said, *I will never be brave enough to work in this place.*

He couldn't have admitted that to Da, although Da had eventually guessed how he felt. Da had taken him to one side and said that everyone was scared at first, but he just had to get over it and not let himself down in front of the other men.

Billy had said nothing, and knew he would never be the man his Da wanted him to be.

What was going to happen now? He hated

the idea of staying on at the shipyard, but he hadn't talked to Ma about it, and with Da gone they might need his wage to help support the family. What else could he do, anyway?

Mabel popped up and pulled his sleeve. 'Ma wants you, Billy,' she piped.

Billy sighed. Apparently Ma could read his mind through several walls and a whole crowd of people. He turned round and headed for the parlour. It looked like Da's workmates wouldn't get their hands on his whiskey just yet.

Ma was sitting on the best sofa with the Reverend Magill. He was sipping tea, a plate of crumbs balanced on one knee. 'The Reverend wanted to see if you're all right,' said Ma, her eyes telling him to *stand up straight and behave.*

'It's a hard thing for a boy to lose his father, Billy,' said the Reverend. 'But at least you have your mother and sisters and a job with good prospects. You must be proud to know you'll be following in your father's footsteps.'

Not if I can help it, thought Billy, seeing in his mind a picture of Da walking along that plank and falling. 'I'll do my best, Reverend,' he said.

'It must be a grand time to be working at the shipyard,' said the Reverend. 'The big ship is a wonder, so it is. You can see it ten streets away.'

'Grand, yes,' said Billy. He did feel proud to be working on the big ship, as everyone called it, even if he only did lots of fetching and carrying.

'And unsinkable, at least according to the newspapers,' said the Reverend. 'Mind you, anyone who knows his classics might call that *hubris*.'

Billy hadn't a clue what he meant. The Reverend often came out with stuff that went over his head. 'The ship's near finished. Then it's sea trials.'

'I know,' said the Reverend. 'I hear they've already taken on some crew. Tom Gibson's son has signed up and he's not much older than you.'

Billy stared at him, then glanced at Ma, their eyes meeting before he looked away.

'Well, thanks for the tea and cake, Mrs Fleming, but I must be off,' the Reverend went on. 'I'll see you and your family next Sunday.'

'Fetch the Reverend his hat, Billy,' said Ma.

Billy saw the Reverend out. But all he could think of was what he'd just heard. Maybe there *was* something else he could do.

Maybe he could get a job on the Titanic.

Chapter Two

The Chief Purser

Reverend Magill had been wrong about one thing, Billy thought as he left for work the next morning. You could see the big ship more than ten streets away. Over the last three years the Titanic had slowly risen beneath a framework of huge gantries until it was a mountain of iron and steel that dominated the city's skyline. From a distance the men working on it looked like ants.

At the end of his street Billy joined those men, a tide of Harland and Wolff workers heading for the shipyard. They were happy, pleased to be in work, proud such a great ship was being built in their city. The Titanic had kept all sorts of trades busy – fitters and welders and platers, of course, and carpenters and decorators and upholsterers since the internal fitting out had begun.

Billy yawned and rubbed his eyes. He had passed a restless, sleepless night, wondering what kind of job there might be for him on the Titanic. It went without saying that the ship would need lots of sailors and stokers for the huge engines. But Billy had heard about the fancy restaurants and beautiful luxury cabins and he hoped there would be better, safer jobs for boys his age.

The tall wrought-iron gates to the shipyard were wide open and Billy went through with everyone else. However, instead of turning to the left and heading in the usual direction, he turned right and made for the long red-brick building that housed the offices. He pushed open the door and went inside.

A polished marble floor stretched before him. Billy walked across it to a wooden counter. A man was leaning on it and writing in a register. 'Excuse me,' said Billy. 'Where are they signing on crew for the Titanic?'

The man pointed his pen at the stairs without looking up. 'Thanks,' said Billy. He climbed the stairs to a landing where a pair of double doors led to a large hall.

Half a dozen tables stood round the walls, men in dark blue uniforms sitting behind each one. There were chairs in front of them for the men being interviewed. More men and a few boys sat on chairs in the middle of the hall, most in caps and working clothes, others in smarter outfits.

Billy was in his working clothes. He hesitated for a moment, then sat beside a boy in a suit.

The boy looked Billy up and down with a smirk and turned to a man on the other side of him to whisper something. They both laughed.

'Next!' called out the man behind the nearest table. The boy in the suit was whispering to his friend again, so Billy stood up and went first. He glanced round as he sat down and saw the boy in the suit glaring at him.

'Name?' said the man at the table. He had a large open face and short dark hair. His uniform was well pressed and his buttons gleamed. On one corner of the table was a brass nameplate that read *Chief Purser H.W. McElroy.*

'Billy Fleming, sir.' Billy put his hands together to stop them trembling.

'What makes you think you could work on the Titanic, Billy?' said Mr McElroy. His accent was English. 'We only want the best crew for her.'

'I'm a hard worker sir, anyone in the shipyard will tell you that, sir.'

'I'm sure you are, but most of the labourers we've seen are only suited to be deckhands or stokers. I'm hiring stewards and waiters and bellboys.'

'Oh, I'm not a labourer, sir,' Billy said quickly. 'I'm an apprentice fitter, but I want to do some other kind of job. Something where you don't have to...'

Billy stopped, uncertain how to continue. He had almost said *something where you don't have to risk your life every day*, but had decided that might not strike the right note. Mr McElroy finished what he was saying for him.

'Where you don't have to get your hands dirty,' he said, and smiled.

'That's it, sir,' said Billy, smiling back. 'I'd like to better myself.'

'Very commendable.'

Mr McElroy paused for a moment and studied him. Billy felt his cheeks turning red, but he held the Chief Purser's gaze. 'Your luck might be in. I'm still looking for a couple of likely lads to be bellboys. It would mean being at the beck and call of wealthy people and doing a lot of fetching and carrying for them. Could you manage all that, Billy?'

'Aye sir, definitely. I wouldn't let you down, sir.'

Mr McElroy tapped his pen on the table. Then he took a sheet of paper from a stack at his elbow and started writing. 'All right, I'll give you a chance. How old are you?' Billy told him. 'I see – you'll need your father's consent.'

'My Da died a week ago, sir. We only buried him yesterday.'

'I'm sorry to hear that, Billy.' Mr McElroy looked up. 'Still got your mother?' Billy nodded. 'She can sign it for you, just here.' He handed Billy the paper and pointed at a line that read

Consent of Parent or Guardian. 'Bring it back tomorrow and we'll see about getting you kitted out. Next!'

Billy stood up and moved away from the table feeling slightly dazed, the paper in his hand. The boy in the suit brushed past him but Billy took no notice. He felt a surge of joy and grinned as he walked out of the hall.

His grin vanished halfway down the stairs. There would be no job if Ma didn't sign the paper. And getting her to do that might not be so easy.

* * *

Ma sat at the kitchen table with a cup of tea and the paper Mr McElroy had given Billy. She had shooed the girls out of the house when Billy told her what he had done, but they had soon sneaked back in. He knew they were on the other side of the kitchen door, their ears pressed up against it.

'Sorry if this is a bit of a shock for you, Ma,' he said.

'It's maybe not so much of a shock as some I've had recently,' said Ma. Billy saw Da's coffin in his mind's eye and felt a wave of guilt. 'Besides,' Ma went on quietly, her eyes fixed on his, 'I was expecting it, so I was.'

'Really?' said Billy, although he wasn't surprised.

'I don't mean you getting a job on the big ship. I knew you wouldn't want to stay on at the shipyard, that's all. Not after your Da was gone.'

Billy didn't know what to say, and was silent for a moment.

'You don't think badly of me, do you, Ma?' he said at last.

'No, I don't, Billy. And I hope you don't think badly of your Da either. He was only trying to do his best for you.'

'It didn't feel like that. Not sometimes, anyway.'

'Well, your Da could be stubborn, and he should have known life is too short for arguing. But I don't mind you leaving the shipyard. I only wish you didn't have to go gallivanting off half way across the world.'

Billy smiled at her, relieved. 'You're always saying half of Ireland has gone to America, Ma. The Titanic's maiden voyage is only to New York. I'll be back in a couple of months. You'll hardly know I've been gone.'

'I doubt that, Billy,' she said. 'I'll miss you every second.'

'Are you sure it's all right, though? What about my wage?'

'Don't you worry about that, Billy. We'll manage. Are *you* sure it's the right thing for you, though? It's a big step for someone your age.'

Billy thought for a second. It was a *huge* step for him, and a scary one. But it would be exciting too. 'Yes, I'm sure,' he said.

'So be it, then,' said Ma, her eyes glistening. 'Now come and give your Ma a hug before I sign your life away on this paper.'

She held him tightly then let him go so that she could wipe her eyes with the wee hanky she always kept tucked up her sleeve. 'I'll still worry about you, so I will,' she said. 'The shipyard is a hard place, but sea voyages can be dangerous too.'

'I'll be fine, Ma. Didn't you hear what the Reverend said? The Titanic is going to be unsinkable, the safest ship there's ever been.'

'I'm glad to hear it,' she said. 'But it still killed your Da.'

Billy frowned. He hadn't thought of it quite that way.

Chapter Three

A Floating City

The next morning Ma went in with Billy and spoke to his foreman. Billy had thought it might be difficult to get out of his apprenticeship, and that Da's workmates might give him a hard time. But it wasn't, and they were pleased for him. 'The Titanic! Good on you, Billy!' one of them said. 'You're better off out of this hellhole. A life of excitement and adventure, that's the ticket.'

'Not *too* much excitement and adventure, I hope,' said Ma, and the men had laughed and clapped him on the back and wished him all the best. Then Ma had gone home to the girls – she had left Ada in charge of the young ones, but they always fought – and Billy went to the offices to find Mr McElroy. He handed over the signed paper, and Mr McElroy smiled and shook his hand.

'Welcome to the Titanic's crew, Billy,' he said. 'You are now an employee of the White Star Line, a fine company and the owners of the greatest ship the world has ever seen. It will be the making of you, I'm sure.'

Over the next few days Billy was instructed in his duties by Mr McElroy, who had plenty of patience, and some of the senior stewards, who had a lot less. He was kitted out with his uniform too, and Ma was impressed by the military-style black trousers, smart red jacket and pillbox hat. But his sisters howled with laughter, and Billy himself thought it would take some getting used to.

He also met the other bellboys. There were ten altogether, most of them decent lads. One, however, was the boy Billy had briefly sat next to on the day he'd got the job. George Anderson was a couple of years older than the rest of them, a big, solid lad with slicked-back black hair. He was very cocky, and had clearly decided that he didn't like Billy Fleming.

Things came to a head on the day Mr McElroy took the bellboys out to the Titanic. The hull had been launched a year ago, and now, less than a week before sea trials, the ship was tied up in the outer dock and accessible only by boat. Billy felt excited as he sat with the other boys in the dinghy. It chugged across the choppy waters, the great ship looming over them, its four funnels outlined against the clear sky, its smooth side a seventy-foot steel cliff.

Suddenly he felt someone cuff his head from behind. His pillbox hat flew off and landed at his feet, and he snatched it up just before it rolled into a pool of dirty water in the dinghy's bilges. Mr McElroy was standing in the bows and looked round at that moment. 'Be careful with that hat, Billy,' he said. 'You'll have to pay for it out of your wages if you lose it.'

Billy quickly put his hat back on. 'Aye sir,' he said. 'I'll be sure to look after it.'

Mr McElroy turned his gaze forwards again, and Billy looked round to see who had knocked off his hat. George Anderson was sitting directly behind him, his arms folded and a smug grin on his face. The other lads laughed and nudged each other. 'I'll be sure to look after it, sir,' George whispered so Mr McElroy wouldn't hear, mocking Billy in a sing-song voice. 'Aye sir, no sir, three bags full, sir.' There was more laughter, the hissing of suppressed giggles.

Billy scowled, but just then the dinghy arrived at the Titanic, clunking against a small platform. A ladder rose from it to a gangway in the hull about thirty feet up. Billy climbed with the others and soon found himself standing at one end of a long corridor inside the great ship. Men bustled past and in and out of the doors lining the corridor, hurrying to get the interior finished. 'Follow me, boys,' said Mr McElroy, and he strode off.

The Chief Purser gave them the full tour of what seemed like a floating city. They started in the depths, in the engine room with its vast boilers and gleaming machinery and giant coal bunkers. Engineers swarmed everywhere, checking pipes and tapping dials, and stokers shovelled coal into the furnaces, ready for the moment when the order would be given to raise steam. From there Mr McElroy took them to see the stores, colossal holds filled with all sorts of supplies for the voyage – thousands of crates and barrels and sacks.

They used the utility stairwells – narrow metal stairs meant for the crew – to move up through the ship, and passed through the third-class accommodation, barely stopping to take in the low-ceilinged dark spaces with their stacks of bunks. Mr McElroy hurried them past the second-class cabins, which were nicer, and more comfortable, than Billy's home and those of his friends.

The first-class cabins and staterooms, however, were something else. Billy had never seen anything like them in his life. A few were enormous, more like the rooms of a great castle or mansion than cabins on a ship. They were all luxuriously fitted out as well, with their own bathrooms and lavatories – no one Billy knew even had a bathroom in their house, let alone a toilet.

'Now, boys,' said Mr McElroy, 'I want you to remember at all times that you'll be serving people who can afford this kind of accommodation. They'll be first-class passengers and they'll expect first-class service.'

'Are we not allowed to help other passengers, sir?' said Billy.

'Don't be daft,' said George. 'Why would you want to?'

Some of the boys sniggered, but stopped when they saw Mr McElroy's frown. 'I doubt you'll have time, Billy. The first-class passengers will keep you pretty busy. And you won't often see anybody from the other classes – the ship has been designed so they're unlikely to meet each other.'

Billy couldn't help thinking that if he and Ma and the girls were emigrating, they'd probably have to travel in third class with the poor people. Mr McElroy had already shown the boys their cabin for the voyage – a cramped space in the crew quarters near the bows, just above more third-class accommodation. What gave rich people the right to sleep in luxury cabins? Billy knew the answer, of course. The difference was money. Rich people could buy anything.

'What about tips, sir?' said George. 'They're allowed, aren't they?'

'You're not allowed to *ask* for a tip,' Mr McElroy said sternly. 'But you can accept one if it's offered. Right, now there's a little more for you to see...'

Mr McElroy led them off again. He showed them the Grand Staircase, the amazing entrance, like something in a palace, that only first-class passengers could use, and pointed out the enormous chandelier hanging from the ceiling high above them, although it would have been pretty hard to miss, Billy thought. They visited the Parisian Café and the first-class restaurant and finally made their way on deck.

The sun was shining, and Billy stood at the handrail, gazing at the shipyard and the narrow streets of Belfast in the near distance, the glittering sea far below him, the misty Mountains of Mourne beyond.

'Right, wait here for me lads,' said Mr McElroy. 'I just need to pick up some papers from my office, then we can go back down to the dinghy.'

He strode off again and the boys relaxed, laughing and joking with each other. Billy glanced at the bridge. He noticed a couple of uniformed officers up there, and realised that the one with a white beard was Captain Smith – he'd seen a picture of him in a newspaper.

Then somebody pushed Billy in the back.

It was George, of course. Billy whipped round and glared.

'I wouldn't stand too close to that handrail if I were you, Billy,' said George. 'You might trip and fall over. It's a long way down, so it is.'

George was grinning, hands on his hips, performing for the other boys. They gathered round as boys do, hoping for trouble, maybe a fight.

Billy clenched his fists and squared up to George. He'd had enough of being pushed around and laughed at and knew there was only one way to end it.

'Oh, so you want to make something of it?' said George, his grin broadening.

Billy was about to hit him – but glanced up at the bridge once more and saw Captain Smith staring down. Billy lowered his fists. How could he get into a fight with the Captain watching? It would be a sure way to lose his job.

'Leave me alone, Anderson,' Billy said and walked off, pushing past.

'Yellow belly!' George said. 'I always knew you were a coward!'

Billy kept right on walking, but he could feel his cheeks burning.

Chapter Four

Score One to Billy

Billy was busy over the next few days, but he still found time to brood on what had happened. He just couldn't get the scene beneath the ship's bridge out of his mind – especially not the word George had used to describe him.

Maybe he *was* a coward. He had ducked a fight, he had backed down in front of the other lads when he should have given George the pasting he deserved.

Of course there had been a good reason – he really didn't want to lose this job. But then perhaps he'd only gone for it in the first place because he was too much of a coward to work in the shipyard.

Billy had been taught at Sunday School that the dead looked down from Heaven on the living. He only hoped Da was keeping more of an eye on Ma and the girls than he was on him.

The Titanic passed its sea trials and the day came when the great ship was due to set sail for Southampton. There it would be handed over officially to the White Star Line and the first passengers would come aboard for the maiden voyage.

The shipyard was decorated with banners and bunting, and a great crowd had gathered in the early April sunshine to see the Titanic off. A brass band on the quayside oom-pah-pahed and made everybody smile.

'Now are you sure you've got everything, Billy?' said Ma. They were on the quayside at the bottom of the crew's gangway into the ship. Ma had put on her best hat for the occasion and the girls were in their best Sunday dresses.

'I'm sure, Ma.' The string of his bulging kitbag cut into his shoulder. Ma had helped him pack, and had made him put in almost all he possessed.

'Well, see you in a few months,' she said. 'Take care of yourself.'

'I will, Ma.' Billy kissed her and his sisters, and suddenly the girls were sobbing again. Little Mabel hung on to Billy until Ma pulled her off.

Billy ran up the gangway and hurried to the boat deck facing the quayside. It was crowded with members of the crew, but he managed to find a space at the handrail beside a lifeboat davit. Each lifeboat was held on a pair of davits, ready to be swung out and lowered to the sea in case of an emergency. The boats were covered with water-tight tarpaulins and smelled of fresh paint.

Far below Billy could see Ma and the girls. They waved, and he waved back. A band was playing and the crowd cheered when the gangways were lowered. The engines throbbed through the deck beneath Billy's boots. After a while the ship gave three great blasts on its foghorn and a gaggle of tugs began to draw it slowly away from the quayside, like dolphins pulling at a giant whale.

Billy waved to Ma and the girls again.

'How sweet,' said a voice behind him. Billy didn't have to look round to know it was George. 'What a lovely family you have there, Billy. Mind you, I bet it's a relief for you to be away from those wee girls, you being a terrible coward and them probably knocking you about all the time. That little one looks a holy terror.'

Billy wanted to punch him, but the same instinct told him this was not the time or the place. He took one last look at the quayside and the crowd and Ma and the girls, then pushed past George and headed to the crew quarters. George said something else, and Billy could feel his smirk burning into his back. There was nothing Billy could do about it. Not at the moment, anyway.

* * *

The sun shone down on them as they sailed out of Belfast Lough and south through the Irish Sea. There were no passengers, and the ship had only a skeleton crew and a temporary skipper – Captain Smith would take full command in

Southampton. Mr McElroy kept the bellboys occupied, using them to run errands all over the ship so they would get to know their way around.

Billy enjoyed the work, but every now and again he would stop by the handrail and gaze out at the sea and sky and the dark smudge of the Welsh or English coastline in the distance. He could hardly believe he was sailing on the most famous ship in the world – that he was actually one of the crew! The whole idea gave him so much pleasure he almost forgot to be homesick.

He wasn't seasick either, unlike most of the bellboys and even some of the stewards and deckhands. 'I'm impressed, Billy,' said Mr McElroy one morning when they were on the foredeck. 'You must be a natural sailor.'

Billy smiled, and turned to look at George. His enemy was leaning over the handrail with a distinctly green tinge to his face, but he still had the energy to glare back at him. *Score one to me*, Billy thought, and walked off.

Docking in Southampton was a great event. They were greeted by a fleet of little boats and tugs and the quayside was even more crowded than in Belfast. The rest of the crew joined the ship, the passengers came aboard, and the bellboys lined up at the top of the Grand Staircase to greet them.

Billy was fascinated to see the rich people he had heard so much about. They wore fine clothes, the men in suits and the ladies in beautiful gowns and fancy hats. But apart from their outfits, Billy thought they looked like anybody else.

'Step lively now, boys,' Mr McElroy said quietly. 'Don't wait to be asked, offer your services. Billy, over here. I've got a special job for you.'

Billy followed Mr McElroy towards a small group of people with two men at its centre. He could sense the other bellboys watching him, George in particular, but he didn't care. In fact he relished being picked out by Mr McElroy.

'This is Mr Ismay, Billy,' said Mr McElroy, nodding at one of the men. Mr Ismay was wearing a dark suit and had a moustache. Its ends were waxed and pointed upwards. 'He runs the company, so he's a very important man.'

'Don't listen to him, Billy,' said Mr Ismay, smiling. 'On this voyage I'm a passenger like any other, and much less important than Mr Andrews here.'

The other man smiled briefly. He was tall and fair, and Billy recognised him immediately. Thomas Andrews was the engineer who had designed the Titanic. He had been pointed out to Billy often enough in the shipyard.

'Oh no, I don't think so,' Mr Andrews said quietly. 'I don't pay the bills.'

'And I've paid some big ones for this ship, I can tell you,' said Mr Ismay. The other men around them laughed politely. 'Well, this won't do,' Mr Ismay continued. 'Lead on, Billy. I'd like to see what kind of stateroom the company's money has paid for. I'll see you at dinner, Andrews. Until later, gentlemen.'

Mr Ismay was pleased with his stateroom and gave Billy a handsome tip, a whole shilling. Billy headed back to the Grand Staircase, pleased as punch.

Two days later they docked in Cherbourg on the other side of the English Channel, but

Billy had no time for even a glimpse of the French port. He was kept busy by the new first-class passengers who came aboard, many of them wealthy Americans on their way home after European tours. There were second-class passengers too, as there had been in Southampton.

It was in Cherbourg that Billy at last encountered some of the third-class passengers. Only a few had come aboard in Southampton, but there were crowds of them waiting on the French quayside. Their clothes were threadbare and patched and they talked in dozens of different languages, none of which Billy could understand. He heard a deckhand say they were from all over Europe and most had probably walked hundreds of miles.

When he went off duty in the afternoon Billy headed for the third-class accommodation near the crew quarters to have a closer look. The whole area was packed with people settling in. Billy noticed a lone mother with four pretty wee girls, all dark, and he felt a sudden pang of homesickness. Like other families, they were housed in a cabin meant for eight people. The four girls were sharing two bunks between them, so there was room in the cabin for five strangers as well.

The youngest girl ran up to him and spoke. 'Sorry,' he said, and shrugged. 'I don't have a clue what you're saying. And I think your ma wants you.'

The mother nodded and rolled her eyes, as if to say, *That one is a handful.*

Billy laughed and nodded back, then turned and headed for his own bunk.

That night he slept better than he had done in weeks.

Chapter Five

A Very Special Job

By the time Billy was on duty again the next morning they were away down the Channel, steaming westwards. They made a last stop, at Queenstown in the south of Ireland, and took on more passengers, almost all third class. Billy stood at the handrail, looking at the town and the road beyond, thinking how strange it was that if he walked due north from here he'd be home in a week.

Within a few hours they were heading out to sea once more, this time on the long Atlantic part of the voyage. The good weather held, although there was more cloud cover now and the temperature seemed to drop by the hour.

'It's always colder on the open sea,' said Mr McElroy when Billy asked him about it. 'Except for Iceland there's no land to stop the freezing winds blowing straight from the Arctic. Don't worry Billy, you'll soon get used to it.'

Billy wasn't so sure, although he did have a thick woollen pea-coat as part of his uniform, the best coat he'd ever had in his life. The bellboys were issued with gloves too, although they were white and more for show than warmth.

Still, things were good, Billy often thought as they sailed on through calm seas, the ocean flat, almost glassy. The great ship moved swiftly, and there was a rumour going round the crew that Mr Ismay had told Captain Smith to make as much speed as possible – it would be good publicity if the ship arrived ahead of schedule. Mr McElroy said that was nonsense and that the engines needed a steady run below top speed to make sure they bedded in.

Not that their speed mattered to Billy. He was enjoying a double life. On duty, he was to be found at the bellboy station outside Mr McElroy's office or running errands. Now everyone was settled in there was a lot less fetching and carrying, although he still had plenty of contact with the first-class passengers. A few were bad-tempered and mean, but most were friendly and having a grand time. Some handed out tips like there was no tomorrow.

Off duty, though, he usually went to check on the woman and her daughters who had come aboard in Cherbourg. With the help of a few other passengers, Billy found out they were Polish, and that the woman's husband was already in America.

'He has a good job,' somebody told Billy. 'They want a better life than the one they had in Poland.'

Billy could understand that, although it seemed a shame they had to leave the home they loved to get on.

Billy came to know the girls' names, although the only one he could say properly was that of the youngest, Anya. Maybe he tried harder with her because she reminded him of his youngest sister, although she wasn't as clingy and whiny as Mabel could be – Anya was very cheeky. She was also prone to wander off on her own and get lost, much to her mother's annoyance.

'There you go,' said Billy, handing Anya over to her mother. It was the afternoon of the second day out of Queenstown and Anya had been missing for over an hour. 'I found the little minx hiding in one of the first-class sitting rooms. I think she likes watching all the rich ladies in their fine clothes.'

The mother told Anya off in a stream of Polish. Billy smiled. Cross mothers obviously looked and sounded the same wherever they were from.

Suddenly Billy felt as if he were being watched himself. He turned round and saw George Anderson in the doorway of the third-class promenade. George smirked at him and walked off, and Billy's heart sank. He had been careful to ensure that none of the other bellboys knew about his visits to Anya and her mother and sisters. George must have somehow cottoned on and followed him down here.

Now George was probably on his way to Mr McElroy, aiming to get Billy in trouble for talking to third-class passengers. Billy sighed and said goodbye to Anya's mother and the girls – Anya giving him a cheeky smile – and trudged off miserably to lie on his bunk, convinced his career with the White Star Line was over and that he would end up back in the shipyard.

A little while later one of the other bellboys came with a summons. Mr McElroy wanted to see him in his office.

Billy knocked on the Chief Purser's door.

'Come in!' said Mr McElroy. The Chief Purser was sitting behind his desk and George was standing in front of it. George looked at Billy and grinned in triumph, as if to say, *I've got you now, Fleming.*

'George has just been telling me he saw you in the third-class promenade, Billy,' said Mr McElroy. 'Fraternising with the passengers. That was the phrase you used, wasn't it, George?'

'Oh aye, Mr McElroy, sir,' said George. 'He was fraternising all right.'

'I can explain, sir...' Billy said, although he wasn't sure that he could.

Mr McElroy held up his hand. 'You don't

have to, Billy,' he said. 'You're off duty, aren't you?' Billy nodded. 'Well, we work you damned hard, and I've always believed that a man who works for a living deserves to spend his leisure time any way he wants, so long as what he does is decent and legal. If you want to make friends with third-class passengers, that's entirely up to you.'

'But sir, you said...' George spluttered.

Mr McElroy frowned. 'Never mind what I said, George. I don't ever want to hear this kind of thing from you again – nobody likes a sneak. Be off with you before I decide the engine room needs another stoker.'

George hurried out, too scared of Mr McElroy to give Billy a glance.

'Thanks, Mr McElroy,' said Billy.

'No need to thank me. You're a good lad and a hard worker, and I know that George and you aren't the best of friends. But he's not as bad as he seems. I think he might even be a decent chap under all that bluster. Now, do you think you can handle another special job for me when you're back on duty?'

Billy grinned. 'Aye sir, you can count on me!'

It was a *very* special job. Billy was to be the messenger between the bridge and the Marconi Room, the cabin on the boat deck where the wireless operators worked. They had the most up-to-date equipment in the world, and could send and receive messages to and from other ships, even America.

'They run the telephone exchange as well,' said Mr McElroy. 'There are telephones for the first-class passengers, but no telephone line between the bridge and the Marconi Room. Seems daft to me but I'm only the Chief Purser, so what do I know? Off you go and introduce yourself to Mr Phillips.'

Billy went to the Marconi Room. He knocked on the door and went in, and was taken aback by how small the cabin was, and how crowded with dials and cables and equipment.

Two men were sitting at a desk, one of them tapping away at the Morse key. Billy was fascinated. The clicking noises it made were a message that was probably being sent to another ship or New York, hundreds of miles away.

The other man looked round at Billy and smiled.

'Mr McElroy sent me,' said Billy. 'I'm to take messages to the bridge.'

'That's good of him,' said the smiling man. He had a light cockney accent, and Billy saw that he was young, in his early twenties. 'You got a name?'

'I'm Billy Fleming, sir. One of the bellboys.'

'I guessed that. Your uniform was a dead giveaway.'

Billy blushed and smiled back at him.

'I'm Junior Wireless Officer Bride, but you can call me Harold, not *sir*. His nibs here is Senior Wireless Officer Jack Phillips.'

'And you can call me *Mr* Phillips, boy,' said the other man, frowning at Harold. He was older, although not much, and looked tired and harassed.

Harold rolled his eyes, making sure Mr Phillips didn't see him. Billy smiled.

'Well, we've got plenty of work for you, Billy,' said Harold. 'Where did you put the sea reports, Jack? We ought to send those up to the bridge at least. Some of them came in hours ago and they've just been sitting on the desk.'

'Is it any wonder?' snapped Mr Phillips. 'I'm so busy sending messages for the first-class passengers I barely have time to think!' He rummaged crossly in a pile of papers, pulled several out and thrust them at Billy. 'Here you are.'

Outside the Marconi Room Billy saw that most of the messages featured the word *iceberg*. He shivered, and hurried up the gangway to the bridge.

Chapter Six

Scribbled Messages

Billy had never been on the bridge before. It occupied the highest part of the ship's forward superstructure, in front of the leading funnel, and was little more than an enclosed space about twenty feet across with a line of windows that gave a view onto the bows and the sea ahead.

There were no doors on either side, and Billy stood at the starboard entrance looking in at the officers on watch.

'Well, are you coming in or not, my lad?' said Mr Wilde, Chief Officer and Captain Smith's second-in-command. 'You'll catch your death out there.'

'Yes sir, sorry sir,' said Billy. 'Mr Phillips gave me these messages for you.'

'Ah, you must be Billy,' said Mr Wilde, with a smile. 'Mr McElroy told me he was going to make you into our messenger boy. We certainly need one.'

Mr Wilde leafed through the messages. There were several other men present – the First Officer, Mr Murdoch, a junior officer Billy didn't recognise, a seaman on lookout duty. A ship's wheel stood in the middle of the bridge, and Billy was puzzled to see that no one was doing any steering. Then he realised the back wall of the bridge was mostly made up of more windows, and beyond those another seaman held a bigger wheel, the true ship's helm.

Billy also noticed several panels on a wall behind the helmsman. One was a diagram of the ship divided into numbered sections, each with a small electric light above it, the whole thing entitled *Watertight Door Indicator Panel*.

Mr Wilde looked up at last from the messages. 'Mr Moody, would you ask the Captain to join us?' he said. 'He should see these.'

The other officer nodded and left the bridge.

'How is it looking, Wilson?' said Mr Wilde.

'No change, sir,' said the lookout. 'Still flat calm as before.'

The sea was smooth and glassy, like the surface of a pond in winter just before it freezes over, Billy thought. But 'flat calm' didn't really describe how beautiful it all was. Titanic's bow pointed directly at the giant red ball of the sun setting on the horizon. The sky was half full of huge heaped clouds, their undersides lit crimson and pink and purple by the dying sun's rays.

Captain Smith arrived on the bridge, Mr Moody in his wake.

'You'd better have a good reason for interrupting my dinner, Mr Wilde,' the captain said.

'Sorry sir,' said Mr Wilde. 'I thought you should see these warnings.'

Captain Smith flicked through the sheaf of papers. 'Nothing to worry about,' he said. 'There are always icebergs at this latitude.'

'But these reports are a few hours old, sir,' said Mr Wilde. 'At our current rate of speed I'm not sure we'll have enough manoeuvrability...'

'Nonsense – this is the Titanic,' said Captain Smith, as if that should settle any argument on the subject. 'Was there anything else?'

Mr Wilde shook his head.

'Excellent. Carry on, Mr Wilde – be sure to keep me informed. If you're still worried, I suggest we adjust our course a few points to the south.'

Captain Smith left the bridge, and Mr Wilde gave a small sigh. Then he turned to Billy. 'Go back to Mr Phillips, Billy, and tell him not to hang on to any iceberg warnings. I want to see them as soon as they're received.'

But Mr Phillips wasn't interested in what Mr Wilde wanted. 'It's all right for *him*, Mr High and Mighty Chief Officer Wilde,' he said. 'I have to deal with all these messages for the first-class passengers. Look at this little lot!' Mr Phillips waved at a heap of scribbled messages in front of him.

'Don't worry, Billy,' said Harold, shaking his head. 'You and I can make sure anything important gets to the bridge. Go and have your dinner now, though.'

Billy went off to the crew dining hall, then called in at the Marconi Room after he'd finished. Harold said that Mr Phillips had got cross with a nearby ship that had kept trying to send him a message. But there were no more iceberg warnings, and it was time for Billy to go off duty.

He went down to check on Anya and her family, and they seemed happy. Some musicians had put together a band. They were all from different countries, but they seemed to get on well enough. The band played wild tunes, and the younger people were dancing in a space at one end of the promenade. Billy watched the fun, but it had been a long day and he soon left.

It was quiet in the bellboys' quarters. Most of the lads were lying on their bunks reading or asleep, a couple talking in hushed voices. Billy lay down on his own bunk and tried to ignore the smell that haunted the crowded areas of the ship, and which seemed to be growing worse the further they got from land – a combination of ocean tang, unwashed feet, and a faint hint of vomit.

George was stretched on his bunk, two over from Billy's. He had looked up when Billy came in, then turned away, ignoring him and concentrating on reading a newspaper Billy knew was four days old.

This is stupid, Billy thought. He remembered Ma saying life was too short for arguing, and thought of his Da. Billy rolled off his bunk and went over to George.

'How long are you going to keep this up, Anderson?' he said.

'What are you talking about, Fleming?' said George, lowering the newspaper. There was a sudden silence in the cabin, the other boys listening.

'You know fine well, and you know where it will end too, so you do.'

George scowled. 'I know where it should end, with me putting you in your place,' he said. 'But I can't lay a finger on the Chief Purser's favourite, can I now? He's bound to take your side.'

Billy sighed. 'I'll fight you any time you like, but I don't see the point. We have to work and live together – so why can't we be friends?'

He held out his hand.

George looked down at it, then up at Billy's face once more. Then he grinned and slowly shook his head.

'Once a coward, always a coward,' he said, and turned to his newspaper again.

Somebody sniggered, and Billy felt stupid standing there with his hand held out. He turned on his heel and got ready for bed, putting on his pyjamas and lying on his bunk beneath the rough blanket that was their only cover.

It was quite late now, after eleven, and soon he was drifting off to sleep, his mind full of images from home, of Ma and his sisters, of Da walking on that plank...

In the dream Billy called out a warning as he always did, but Da never heard him, and Billy had to watch as he tumbled down, although Billy usually woke up before Da hit the ground. But this time the dream ended with a bump that Billy felt in his whole body, and he realised he was awake, his eyes open. There was a loud scraping noise too, the whole cabin reverberating and shaking.

'What the hell is that?' said someone. 'Have we hit something?'

'Don't be daft,' somebody else said. 'What could we hit out here? We're in the middle of the Atlantic, for Heaven's sake, nothing but sea for miles.'

Billy thought of the warnings from the Marconi Room. *Icebergs*. He sat up, anxiety fluttering in his stomach. Some of the boys were out of their bunks and everyone listened, but the scraping ended as suddenly as it had begun.

'The engines have stopped,' said George, and the boys looked at each other, even more puzzled. They had grown used to the constant throbbing in every part of the ship. To Billy it had felt like the pulse of a living thing, and now the ship was strangely inert, the bunks and decks and bulkheads suddenly stilled.

He jumped up, pulled off his pyjamas and started putting on his uniform. 'Well, I don't know about anyone else,' he said. 'But I'm off to find out what's going on.' Soon he was on his way to the boat deck, the rest following.

They found themselves in the middle of a strange scene. Big chunks of ice were scattered over the boat deck. A few deckhands were kicking them around like footballs, their laughter cutting through the cold night air. Billy looked beyond them, and what he saw chilled his blood in more ways than one.

A colossal iceberg loomed over the ship, almost close enough to touch.

Chapter Seven

Argument on the Bridge

Billy and the other bellboys went to the handrail and looked out over the sea, the blaze of light from Titanic's portholes and deck lamps casting a glow for hundreds of feet around the ship. The iceberg was enormous, a craggy white mountain that glittered beneath the stars of a moonless sky. Even so, most of it was below the surface, a massive, ghostly presence in the water. Ship and iceberg drifted apart, the sea quietening in the growing gap between them.

'Will you look at the size of that!' said somebody, awe-struck.

'What kind of damage would hitting an iceberg do to the ship?' said another voice.

Billy turned round and saw it was a worried-looking George.

'They're trying to find out,' said the boy who had spoken first. He nodded in the direction of a group of men at the handrail closer to the bows.

Billy was very glad to see Mr Andrews there with them. They were lucky to have him aboard. He had designed the ship, so he should know how to deal with any damage caused by colliding with an iceberg.

But as Billy watched, the fluttering of anxiety in his stomach grew worse. Mr Andrews's face grew grim as he peered over the handrail, and he soon hurried away below deck.

Some passengers had come out to point at the iceberg and the chunks of ice on the deck. They were in high spirits, as if what had happened was some kind of entertainment laid on just for them by the White Star Line.

After a while Mr McElroy appeared. 'Glad to see you boys up and ready,' he said. He was smiling and seemed as calm as ever. 'Best if you wait at the bellboy station in case you're needed for anything. Billy, I want you to come with me to the bridge.'

It was quite crowded on the bridge. Most of the ship's officers were there, a dozen serious-looking men, a couple still hurriedly doing up the buttons of their uniform jackets.

Captain Smith stood slightly apart with Mr Ismay.

'This is a poor show, Captain Smith,' Mr Ismay said, like a parent telling off a child. But then Mr Ismay was Captain Smith's employer, Billy thought, so perhaps he was entitled to speak to him that way. 'I fail to understand how you managed to hit an iceberg in the middle of the Atlantic. Aren't you supposed to have lookouts for this sort of thing? Surely you should have seen it.'

'Of course we have lookouts, Mr Ismay,' the Captain said stiffly. 'They spotted the iceberg, but it was too late. Isn't that so, Mr Wilde?'

'That's right, sir,' said Mr Wilde. 'We might have hit it head on if we hadn't taken any evasive action. But our speed made things rather difficult.'

'Don't try to blame me for this,' snapped Mr Ismay. 'I might have suggested that a swift crossing wouldn't be a bad thing, but you're the people we actually employ to sail the ship. Weren't there any warnings? Isn't that what the Marconi Room is for? All that equipment certainly cost a pretty penny.'

Billy saw Mr Wilde glance at the Captain. 'Yes, there were some warnings,' said Mr Wilde. 'Our new messenger brought them up earlier.' He nodded in Billy's direction and everyone turned to stare at him. 'For some reason they'd been held back, and I thought the Captain ought to see them.'

'Is that correct, Captain?' said Mr Ismay. 'You saw the warnings?'

'I did, Mr Ismay,' the Captain said even more stiffly. 'In my judgement there was nothing to worry about, although I did order a course correction.'

'Your judgement was wrong,' said Mr Ismay. He moved to the windows and looked out. Silence fell on the bridge, and Billy could feel the embarrassment in the room. Beside him

Mr McElroy was frowning, his mouth a tight line.

Eventually Mr Ismay turned round. 'Well, what's done is done,' he said. 'There will have to be an inquiry, of course, and you will have to take the consequences, Captain Smith. But the important thing is that the passengers shouldn't be inconvenienced. How soon can we get under way again?'

'I'm afraid the Titanic won't be getting under way at all, Mr Ismay.'

Mr Andrews had arrived on the bridge, and everyone now turned to stare at him. Billy suddenly had the feeling that he should remember this scene, these men standing on the bridge of a great ship, their faces pale and anxious, their breath steaming in the cold air. It was the kind of picture the Bible at Sunday School had been full of, a grim-faced prophet of doom bringing bad news.

'What are you talking about, Andrews?' said Mr Ismay. 'We can't just sit here. It's vital that we make good time. A lot of investment depends on it.'

'I'm afraid the damage to the hull is very serious,' said Mr Andrews. 'The front four compartments are flooded, and compartments five and six are already beginning to fill. The bilge pumps can't deal with the flow.'

'I ordered the watertight doors of the first four compartments to be closed,' said one of the officers. 'We could simply do the same for five and six.'

Billy glanced at the panel behind the helmsman. Sure enough, the little lights over each of the first four panels now glowed red. But those compartments made up a large part of the ship – a quarter of the whole, Billy now realised, seeing that the last compartment of all, the stern section, was number 16.

'It wouldn't make any difference, Mr Murdoch,' said Mr Andrews. 'There's a long gash in the forward part of the hull and the sea is getting into five and six directly. You'll notice that the ship is already beginning to tip at the bow.'

All heads turned to look at the bow, and Billy could see immediately that he was right.

The front part of the ship was leaning slightly downward.

'Good God, man,' murmured Mr Ismay. 'What are you saying?'

'This ship was designed to stay afloat with four compartments flooded,' said Mr Andrews. 'But we can't stop the rest flooding too. Once six is filled to the level of its top bulkhead the water will start flooding into seven, then eight, and so on. What I'm saying, Mr Ismay, is that the Titanic is going to sink.'

There was a sharp, collective intake of breath from the men on the bridge. Immediately voices were raised in dissent.

'You can't be serious! That's impossible,' said Captain Smith. 'This is the Titanic, the world knows she's designed to be unsinkable.'

'I wish that were true,' Mr Andrews said quietly. 'But I'm afraid it isn't. Perhaps it was *hubris* even to think such a thing in the first place.'

There it was again, Billy thought, the same word Reverend Magill had used after Da's funeral. 'What does that word mean, sir?' Billy asked.

'It means arrogant pride – the kind that's doomed to fail,' said Mr Andrews, their eyes meeting. 'It's ancient Greek. There's a line in the Bible that says the same thing, but at greater length – *pride goeth before destruction, and a haughty spirit before a fall.*'

'Is it possible that you might be wrong, Andrews?' said Mr Ismay.

Just then there was a creaking, groaning noise from deep inside the bowels of the ship, almost as if the Titanic herself was answering Mr Ismay's question.

'No,' said Mr Andrews with absolute finality.

'How long do we have?' said Captain Smith, his face stricken.

'According to my calculations, about an hour. Two hours at the most,' said Mr Andrews.

'And according to *my* calculations,' said Mr Wilde, 'we only have enough space in the lifeboats for half the passengers. What about the rest?'

'We'll worry about that in due course,' Mr Ismay said briskly, avoiding Mr Wilde's gaze. 'There are some very important people on this ship who must be given priority. Well, Captain Smith? What are you waiting for? Are you going to give the order to abandon ship, or do I have to do it for you?'

Captain Smith stared at him for a moment, his jaw set.

'You heard Mr Ismay, gentlemen,' he said at last. 'Mr Wilde, get the lifeboats launched. Mr McElroy, have the wireless operators send a distress signal – there might be some ships nearby. The rest of you know your duties. May God have mercy on us all.'

'Come on, Billy,' said Mr McElroy, and they hurried off the bridge. Billy looked round and saw the Captain standing alone, his fists clenched.

Chapter Eight

Rich Man's Rules

Billy shivered as he scurried along behind Mr McElroy on the way to the Marconi Room, and he knew it wasn't only because of the cold. The night air was freezing, but it was fear that made him tremble.

It was as if Mr Andrews had just announced the end of the world. For the last three years Billy had watched the big ship growing in the shipyard until it was this vast structure of iron and steel that felt so solid beneath his feet, and now it was doomed.

Suddenly he remembered what Ma had said about the ship – *it killed your Da*. She was right about voyages being dangerous, too. Billy knew that people drowned when ships went down. He couldn't help wondering what Ma would feel if the ship that had taken her husband's life took her son's as well. Come to think of it, he wouldn't be too happy about it himself.

'Was Mr Wilde right about the lifeboats, Mr McElroy?' Billy said.

'I'm afraid so, Billy. The company decided we only needed the minimum number of boats required by the Board of Trade, and that was sixteen, with four collapsible boats as well. And I think he was being optimistic about how many passengers they'll take. I have a feeling it will be a lot less than half.'

'What about using lifebelts, sir? Couldn't everyone else just swim?'

'They won't last long in the water, Billy. You'd maybe have a few minutes before you froze to death.'

Billy glanced at him, but he didn't get the chance to ask any more questions – they had arrived at the Marconi Room. Both operators were there, and both were shocked by the news they brought.

'Are you sure?' said Mr Phillips. 'We felt the bump all right, but it didn't seem serious enough to sink the ship.'

'According to Mr Andrews it was, and he should know,' said Mr McElroy. 'Now, let's get that distress call out. Are there any ships in the vicinity?'

'There are,' said Harold. 'But we don't know how close.'

'You'd better see if you can find out,' said Mr McElroy. 'We'll need some help. I'll send Billy back in ten minutes to take any messages to the bridge.'

'Yes sir!' said Mr Phillips, tapping at the Morse key already.

'Keep your chin up, Billy!' said Harold. 'We're not dead yet!'

Back at the bellboy station the boys were chattering, laughing and fooling about in the usual way. But they fell silent and rose to their feet when the grim-faced Mr McElroy came in with Billy behind him.

Moments later the boys looked as stricken as Captain Smith. George's face was deathly white, his expression one of terror, but it gave Billy no pleasure to see him like that.

'I won't lie to you boys, we're in a desperate fix,' said Mr McElroy. 'But it's our duty to assist the passengers in any way we can. And to begin with, I want you out on the boat deck helping them into lifeboats.'

The boat deck was as busy as Billy had ever seen it. Groups of seamen were working on the lifeboats, stripping off the tarpaulins and getting ready to winch them down into the sea. More seamen and deckhands were stationed by the gangway doors telling groups of passengers where to go. A couple of officers were shouting orders at the men, and Billy could see they were anxious. But as yet they seemed to be concealing their worries from the passengers.

'What is this all about, young man?' said an elderly lady, addressing Mr Lightoller, the Second Officer. She was clearly wealthy, and also very cross at having been woken up, told to put her fur coat on over her nightdress and go up on deck in the freezing night air. 'Is it some kind of drill? I really don't think this is the kind of thing I should have to put up with, not at my age.'

'Just a precaution, ma'am,' said Mr Lightoller. 'Hurry along, please.'

Mr McElroy detailed the boys off to various parts of the boat deck, and Billy soon found himself carrying a bag for a rich American lady. They were in a queue shuffling towards a lifeboat, but there seemed to be a problem.

'What are you doing, you damned fool?' an officer suddenly yelled at a seaman. 'You can't start lowering the boat till the passengers are in it!'

'Sorry, sir,' said the seaman. 'But I've only lowered it a little way.'

'Say, are we going to get in this boat or not?' said a man beside Billy, the husband of the lady whose bag Billy was carrying. 'I'm freezing my butt off standing here in just my PJs and my suit coat.'

'Language, Wilbur!' snapped his wife, and the passengers around them laughed, seemingly unworried. 'I'm sure they're doing what they can.'

Another seaman opened a small gate in the handrail above the lifeboat, and he and Billy began to help passengers climb down into it.

A moment later Billy heard a whooshing noise and he looked up. A rocket rose into the black sky above the ship and exploded into a starburst. 'That's a distress flare,' somebody said, and the words seemed to send a shiver of fear through the crowd.

'Right, that's it, stand back everybody!' yelled the officer. Billy could hear an edge of panic in his voice. 'Lower away! Move on to the next boat, men...'

'But that boat is less than half full!' a man said.

Billy peered over the handrail and saw that he was right. The lifeboat was descending slowly to the dark sea below, jerking occasionally as the winches snagged, its benches half empty.

'Can't be helped!' said the officer. 'There's plenty of room for everyone!'

Billy knew that wasn't true, but he didn't think it was his place to tell the passengers. He moved away, intent on finding someone else to help.

People pushed past him roughly, voices were raised, and he realised things were beginning to get out of control. That was no great surprise. The ship was shuddering and groaning and creaking and the bow had tilted down much more noticeably. A second distress rocket went up and a woman screamed.

Billy knew how she felt. He was trying hard not to think about what would happen to him if he ended up being one of the many people who didn't make it into a lifeboat. But he was definitely scared, panic clawing at his insides.

'There you are, Billy!' said Mr McElroy, emerging from the crowd. 'Go back to the Marconi Room and see if there are any messages for the bridge.'

'Aye, sir!' said Billy, and ran off, dodging people going the other way. The only messages were from ships that were too far away to help. On the bridge, Captain Smith read them silently and turned to look down at the chaos on the boat deck. Billy waited, but the Captain said nothing. So Billy left, heading for another lifeboat – and saw something very disturbing on the way.

Three seamen with their arms linked were standing across a door to a gangway that led below. They were facing outwards, and behind them was a heaving mass of humanity, third-class passengers trying to get out on deck.

'Why are you holding us back, you rogues?' roared a man on the gangway. He had a strong southern Irish accent and was pushing against the seamen.

'Orders, chum,' yelled one of the seamen. 'Women and children first.'

The Irishman swore at him. 'That's a joke,' he said. 'I can see men getting into those boats as well as women and children. That'll be the first-class men, though. And there are plenty of women and children down here too!'

Billy remembered what Mr Ismay had said, that the important people on the ship should have priority. It didn't seem right, and it was clear others agreed.

'Aye, it's rich men's rules on this ship, right enough,' yelled another man in the crowd. 'But why should we drown so the rich can live? Come on, lads!'

With a great roar the crowd pushed the seamen aside and burst out. Billy quickly stood back, not wanting to be trampled in the rush as at least one of the seamen had been. There were more shouts and screams from the direction of the nearest lifeboat, and Billy wondered what to do. Then he glimpsed Anya's mother emerging from the gangway with her daughters.

But when Billy looked more closely, he saw that only three of the girls were there. Anya wasn't with them, and her mother was in tears.

'What's happened?' said Billy, hurrying over to her. 'Where's Anya?' His questions were answered with a stream of incomprehensible Polish, but he soon got the gist of it. Anya was up to her old tricks and had wandered off again.

And now she was lost somewhere on the sinking ship.

Chapter Nine

Cold Water Rising

Billy tried to find out more from Anya's mother, perhaps get a clue as to where she had seen Anya last, but it was impossible. Language was a barrier between them and there was nobody to translate. Those around them were all too concerned for their own safety and that of their families to stop and help any strangers. The more the ship creaked and groaned and shuddered, the more steeply the bow tilted downwards, the greater the panic and chaos.

He knew Anya's mother was in an impossible situation. She couldn't search for Anya with the other girls, and she couldn't go off and leave them alone. They had to stick together, which meant there was only one thing for it.

'Don't worry, I'll find her!' Billy said, pointing to himself and then down the gangway. Anya's mother seemed to understand, and nodded.

Billy smiled at her and the girls, all of them frightened and crying and clinging to their mother. 'Wait here!' he yelled, pointing at the deck where they were standing. Anya's mother nodded again, and Billy decided that had to be good enough.

He turned and descended into the ship, hurrying down the metal stairs of the gangway, leaving the sound of chaos behind him. The best place to look would be the first-class lounges, but the gangway would take him past the third-class cabin area where Anya and her family had their bunks. Billy decided it would do no harm to check in there first, just in case Anya had gone back.

The gangway also took Billy past his own quarters. He glanced through the door and stopped. George was huddled on his bunk with his back to him.

'What do you think you're playing at, Anderson?' Billy said, surprised. 'You should be up on deck helping the passengers. You heard Mr McElroy.'

George jumped to his feet and stood between the rows of bunks. 'I'm... I was just...' he said, wiping his face on his sleeve. He took a deep breath and Billy could see his eyes were red and his cheeks damp. 'Er... I might ask you the same thing, Fleming,' George said, visibly cranking himself up into indignation and bluster, trying to conceal the fact that he had been crying by going onto the attack. 'Hoping to find something to steal while everyone else is busy?'

'Watch your mouth,' said Billy. 'That's more your kind of stunt.'

'You watch your own mouth,' said George, his voice unsteady. 'I can't have you going around saying things like that. It's time I put you in your place.'

Billy was about to tell him not to be so stupid, but George punched him, his fist landing squarely on Billy's jaw. The iron taste of blood filled Billy's mouth and his head rang like a bell.

But he got his fists up and managed to block the next few blows. George was swinging like a madman, screaming in rage.

Billy gave ground slowly, still blocking George's punches. Here he was on the back foot again, but hadn't that been the way of it since he and George had met? Billy had offered friendship and had it thrown back in his face, and now something snapped inside him.

He brushed aside another wild swing and hit out himself. His knuckles connected with George's cheekbone and the older boy reeled backwards, shocked by Billy's onslaught. Billy drove his left fist hard into George's stomach and George fell to the deck like a sack of potatoes. He clutched his gut, curled up tight against a bulkhead and started sobbing.

'I can't swim,' George whimpered. 'I can't even swim.'

Billy lost any remaining patience he might have had. He grabbed George's collar and dragged him to his feet. 'You'll freeze to death in the water long before you drown, you idiot,' he hissed, leaning in close. 'And I don't care how scared you are, or how much you hate me. A little girl is going to die if I don't find her. You help me, or I'll send you straight to hell myself.'

'But what can we do?' said George, his face pale and desperate. 'We're going to die! One of the seamen told me there's not enough room in the lifeboats. People like you and me will be at the back of the queue.'

'Maybe so,' said Billy, his anger draining away. He remembered what Mr McElroy had said about George being a decent chap under all his bluster, and now he could see that George was just a scared boy, like Billy himself – the only difference being that George obviously couldn't handle his fear.

'Maybe *we* are going to die,' Billy went on. 'But at least we can try to save somebody else, a little girl. Or do you just want to stay here feeling sorry for yourself?'

George rubbed the tears from his eyes once more and took another deep breath, his whole body shuddering. He breathed out, and it was like a balloon deflating, any remaining bluster seeping away. 'No, I don't,' he said quietly.

'Well, get a grip on yourself,' said Billy. 'We don't have a moment to lose.'

* * *

There was no one in Anya's cabin or in the third-class area when they arrived. The space that had been so full of life before was empty, luggage, clothes and papers strewn where fleeing passengers had discarded them.

The deck seemed even more tilted here than elsewhere, perhaps because they could see more of it, thought Billy. Half a dozen bottles had rolled down and were clanking against a steel bulkhead.

'Search everywhere,' Billy told George. 'Under the bunks, in the chests...'

He hadn't realised just how big the third class accommodation was. When it had been full, the men, women and children had been packed in like sardines. Now Billy called Anya's name and his voice echoed back to him.

The two boys tore through the entire space. They checked the cubicles in the shared washrooms, and looked in every corner, every nook and cranny.

'She's not here,' George said finally.

'She must be up in first class,' said Billy.

'First class? But she's not allowed…'

'Doesn't matter now, does it? Come on.'

They ran as fast as they could through the ship. Several times they heard snatches of wild shouting and yelling coming down from the boat-deck through open doorways. Even though he couldn't make out any of the words, Billy could tell everyone up there was even more scared and angry than before.

The ship groaned and shuddered, and occasionally they passed people running in the opposite direction, most of them wild-eyed and panicking.

Eventually they came to the first-class areas. They burst through a set of doors and the Grand Staircase was in front of them. It looked just as it had before, and for a moment Billy simply couldn't believe that all of this could sink. Then he looked up and saw the huge chandelier hanging at an angle, pointing towards the bow.

It was going to be under water. Soon.

He dashed towards the lounge he'd found Anya in before and called out to her. Glass crunched under his feet. He looked down and saw the remains of an expensive bottle of whisky, its dark contents staining the rich carpet.

'Here, Fleming,' George shouted suddenly. He had crouched down by a table and was peering underneath it. 'It's all right, sweetheart. We're here to help.'

Billy ran over and knelt down too. Anya was on the floor, hugging her knees, her big eyes wet with tears. He held out a hand and tried his best to smile.

'There you are, Anya!' he said softly. 'We've been looking for you.'

She stared at him solemnly, then took his hand and crawled out. When they stood, she wrapped her arms round Billy's waist and squeezed him as if she'd never let go. He picked her up and she buried her small face in his neck.

They jogged back out of the lounge the way they had come and took the Grand Staircase up towards the boat deck. The corridors were empty but they were close enough to hear the chaos on deck. They were nearly there.

At last they turned a corner – and ran into a metal gate that had been pulled across the passage. Billy put Anya down and tried to move it aside, but it was firmly locked into place. Some overly efficient steward must have pulled it across to keep the first-class staterooms safe from thieves, Billy thought. He could see the exit to the boat deck no more than a few yards away.

'Maybe we can force it,' said George, rattling the gate.

'No chance,' said Billy. 'We need another way out.'

'We can get to the second-class exit if we go back.'

'Lead the way,' said Billy, scooping Anya up again.

They moved back through the corridors and down the Grand Staircase once more. Billy heard a splash when he jumped off the last step. First his toes, then his heart froze as he watched the cold water rising around his feet.

Chapter Ten

Death Trap

The water was flowing towards them along the floor of the passage – their only route to salvation although it was sloping downwards – and Billy could feel the level was already above his ankles.

'I think we need to get a move on,' he said, holding Anya tight against him. He could feel her shivering with cold.

'I was about to say the same thing myself, so I was,' muttered George.

They started to run, but the freezing seawater slowed them down. Soon it was up to their knees and they had to wade. Bits of paper floated past them and Billy was surprised to see it was money, maybe hundreds of pounds. George wanted to stop and grab some, but there was no time.

Billy forged on, his back aching from carrying Anya, and George followed, shaking his head.

Soon they had left the first-class areas behind. They rounded a corner, and now Billy could see where the water was coming from. A little way ahead a bulkhead door had bulged inwards, and water was spraying out round the entire frame, the metal squeaking and groaning as if it were in pain. Suddenly a rivet shot out and hit the opposite wall of the passage with a dull clang.

The boys looked at each other and pushed on, crouching down, as there were rivets all round the door. Another shot out as they passed it, just missing them, but for a second Billy thought they were safe. Then there was an almighty bang, louder than anything he'd heard in the shipyard, and he was thumped in the back by a freezing torrent. The door had been blown off completely.

Billy was washed along by the force of the unleashed water. He tried to hold on to Anya but he was slammed into a bulkhead and she was torn from his grasp. He grabbed another door frame and it took all his strength to get his head up for a great, gulping breath. There was less than a foot of air between the corridor's ceiling and the flood, and the water was rising relentlessly.

George was whipped past, and Billy reached out to grab his arm and pulled the other boy to him. Billy's fingers slipped off the door frame and the torrent swept the boys further down the passage. Billy hit something, his back grinding into what felt like metal steps, and realised they were in one of the utility stairwells. They could get up on deck from here.

But what about Anya?

George coughed water from his lungs and clawed his way onto the steps. The agonising cold spread through Billy's bones, sending icy jolts of pain through every muscle. He dragged himself up beside George and the two boys lay panting on the metal stairs, the water lapping at their boots.

But Billy knew he couldn't stay there long. He helped George up the next flight of steps and sat him down next to another bulkhead door that was still half open.

'I'm going back for Anya,' Billy said, stripping off his sodden jacket.

George stared at him in disbelief. 'But she must be dead!' he said.

'Maybe not,' Billy said, pulling off his boots and trying to ignore how cold he felt. 'There's a chance she might be in one of the cabins off the corridor.'

'You're mad,' said George, his teeth chattering. 'Even if she's alive, you'll never make it. The corridor will be full to the ceiling by now, and this stairwell is a death trap. We won't get out once the water rises and closes the door.'

'Then you'd better keep it open, Anderson,' Billy said quietly.

They stared at each other for a moment. George nodded.

'I... I'll do my best, so I will,' he said, hugging himself.

'That's all any of us can do,' said Billy, remembering something he'd heard Reverend Magill say in a sermon. 'See you in a wee while.'

Billy turned and went down the steps. The level had risen at least a foot while they had been talking, and he tried not to think about that. He felt chilled to the bone, his pulse beat a tattoo in his ear and he was terrified – he knew that he would have to swim further under water than he had ever done in his life. And then he would have to swim the same distance back again. He took a deep breath, gritted his teeth – and plunged into the freezing water.

His heart pounded as the bitter cold clutched at his body, but he pulled himself through the door and swam into the corridor again. The ceiling lights glowed fuzzily through the water. Billy suddenly wondered why the ship's electrics hadn't failed – and hoped it wouldn't happen just yet. Swimming in freezing water while he held his breath was bad enough. Doing it in the dark would be a nightmare, and one he probably wouldn't wake up from.

Billy kicked on, heading the way they'd come. He passed open doors and quickly checked the cabins, but they were all empty. Floating through the empty, beautiful ship was like being in a strange dream, although soon his lungs were burning. He kept his mouth shut tight, knowing he had to hold on to what little air he had left. The corridor was getting darker. No, not the corridor – his vision was fading. His head pounded. He was going to drown down here...

Then suddenly through another door he caught sight of a pair of small legs. He swam into the cabin, a large one, and pushed himself up. His head burst out of the water and he smacked into the ceiling.

There were barely two inches of air, but he gulped in a breath and felt himself coming back to life.

Anya was beside him, clinging to a light fitting on the wall. Her lips were blue, but she chattered excitedly in Polish and was clearly very happy to see him. She threw her arms round his neck and squeezed tight.

'Don't you worry, Anya,' he said. 'I'm going to save you.'

He pointed down into the water. He pointed at both of them and then down again, trying to mime what they were going to do.

At first she shook her little head, eyes wide with terror, and Billy thought he would have to drag her with him kicking and screaming. But then she seemed to calm down, and before long she was nodding, letting him know she would do what he wanted.

'You're a good girl, Anya, even if you do run off,' Billy said, smiling at her. 'And I think you're probably a darn sight braver than I'll ever be.'

He put one arm round her and mimed taking a deep breath. Anya did as she was told, and Billy plunged them under the water before she had a chance to change her mind. Billy knew where he was going and he wasn't about to let down the little girl in his arms.

Even so, his chest was in agony by the time they reached the stairwell and he started swimming upwards. Then he saw the one thing he had been scared of. The rising water had covered the bulkhead door – and it was closed. Billy kicked against it, but all he did was stub his toe.

He looked up. There was only more water above, no pocket of trapped air. He felt the awful pressure in his lungs, the desperate need to take a breath. Anya clung on even more tightly and stared at him with the fear of death in her child's eyes, her cheeks puffed out. She shook her head again and a stream of bubbles burst from her mouth. Her grip on him began to slacken and her eyes closed.

She was going to die because he hadn't saved her. It was his fault...

Suddenly there was a screeching noise and Billy felt himself being sucked towards the door. The end of a metal pole had appeared at one edge and he realised someone had pushed it through from the other side to lever the heavy door open. The water was flooding out, pulling Billy and Anya with it.

The door inched wider and Billy tried to help, pulling at the door with his free hand, straining with all his might, feeling as if he was fighting the force of the whole Atlantic Ocean. Then with a rush they were washed out into a corridor beyond.

George stood over them, breathing heavily, still gripping the pole.

'I'm sorry, so sorry, I couldn't stop it closing, I thought you were a goner,' he said, his face full of anguish. 'I had to go and find something to get it open.'

He pulled the pole out and the pressure of the water in the stairwell instantly slammed the door shut with a clang. Billy rolled over to check on Anya. She lay still, her face deathly white, her eyes still shut, her lips bluer than before.

'Oh, dear God,' whispered George. 'Is she…?'

Billy couldn't believe it. He'd been so close.

He reached out to grab her, shake her till she woke up. Instead, he clumsily slammed into her chest, landing hard on her with his shoulder. She coughed and retched, then moaned.

'She's alive!' shouted George. 'You did it, Fleming! You saved her!'

But had he? For all he knew they might still be trapped.

Chapter Eleven

First Class Only

Anya retched some more, but she seemed to recover well enough. If she was anything to go by, Billy thought, these Poles must be pretty tough people. But the three of them were shivering, their clothes were soaked, and Billy wondered how much longer they could keep going.

They had to get up on deck.

'Any idea where we are?' he said, looking round, his teeth chattering.

'In the middle of the ship,' said George. 'It's all first class here.'

A long corridor stretched away, cabin doors lining both sides. It felt strange to be in a part of the ship that was still dry and looked relatively normal. 'Right, this way,' said Billy, trying to sound confident that he knew what to do. He picked Anya up once more and hurried off, Billy following close behind.

'Hang on a second, Fleming,' George said when they hadn't gone far. He had stopped by an open door and was grinning. 'Fancy a change of clothes?'

Billy and Anya peered through the door. Beyond it was one of the first-class suites, and it was clear its occupants had left in a hurry. Two huge travelling trunks stood open on the carpet, clothes of all kinds spilling from them.

'I'd like to feel drier, so I would,' said Billy, grinning now too. 'And it would be good for Anya to get a bit warmer. But we'll have to be quick.'

Billy and George tore through the luggage, examining clothes and discarding them until they found what they wanted. Within minutes Anya was swaddled in a nightshirt and a thick pullover. Billy shed what was left of his uniform and pulled on some trousers and a pullover, both too big for him. George did better – one of the former occupants of the cabin must have been more his size.

Suddenly the deck beneath their feet juddered and they heard a grinding noise louder than anything they'd heard before. The cabin's lights flickered and went out, plunging them into darkness. Anya squealed and held on to Billy's leg, and George yelled in panic. For a brief moment Billy was convinced they were finished. They'd never find their way up on deck in the dark. But then the lights flickered into life again and they all breathed huge sighs of relief.

'Come on,' said Billy. 'We are *definitely* running out of time!'

They left the cabin and headed along the corridor until they came to a gangway that led upwards. Anya seemed to be getting heavier, and Billy puffed and panted as they climbed the steps. His arms and shoulders ached so badly he didn't think he could carry her much further. They went up one flight, then another, Billy worrying all the while that they'd find another gate at the top.

But they didn't. The doors were open and unblocked and Billy, Anya and George emerged onto the boat deck not far from where Billy had begun his descent into the bowels of the ship earlier.

Things had changed a great deal, though, and for a moment Billy just stood and stared at the incredible scene before them, Anya still clinging to him, her arms tight round his neck.

The ship's bow was completely submerged and the sea lapped at the windows of the bridge. There were people everywhere, some stumbling around as if in a daze, some running, many of them shouting the names of family or friends or screaming in despair.

The deck tilted downwards steeply, and Billy saw a man trip and fall then roll head over heels until he crashed into a bulkhead.

Further along, the band from one of the first-class lounges was playing a haunting, sad tune, five men in evening dress with violins, their pale faces rapt.

'God, it's like a madhouse,' George said, his voice hushed.

Suddenly, with a familiar whoosh, another distress rocket rose into the night sky and exploded. The starburst lit the sea in a great ring round the ship and Billy saw at least half a dozen lifeboats moving steadily away over the dark water, maybe more. But that was on this side, he realised. There were only sixteen lifeboats in total – so most of them might already have been launched.

'I think we'd better find your Ma and sisters, Anya,' Billy said.

Anya's mother, however, wasn't where Billy had told her to wait. Anya burrowed into Billy's neck and started to cry. He tried to comfort her, then caught sight of her mother and sisters standing at the rear of a crowd further along the deck.

'Hey, over here!' he yelled, and Anya's mother whipped round, her face full of joy. She ran to Billy, Anya's sisters clinging to her skirts.

Anya leapt out of Billy's arms and into her mother's. There was a lot of weeping and wailing and hugging and streams of Polish. Anya's mother was sobbing with joy to have her daughter back, although she was obviously surprised to see her in such strange clothes, and at one point Billy was sure she gave Anya a telling-off.

That would be for getting lost in the first place, Billy realised, and smiled when he thought his own Ma would do the same.

Then Anya's mother grabbed Billy and started planting kisses all over his face. Anya was almost crushed between them and George stood back, laughing.

'You've made a friend for life there, so you have, Billy Fleming,' he said. 'In fact, if she wasn't already married, I'd say you were in with a chance.'

'You don't know what you're talking about,' muttered Billy, trying to push Anya's mother off. He could feel himself blushing despite the bitter cold. 'I can't understand why the blasted woman is making such a fuss of me.'

'Well, you did just save her daughter's life,' said George.

'Not yet,' said Billy, freeing himself at last. 'The job's only half done. We need to get them in a lifeboat or we might as well not have bothered.'

George stopped laughing and that anguished look returned to his face. Anya's mother sensed the change in mood. She said something to Billy, a single word, then tugged his arm and pointed at the crowd where he had spotted her. She spoke again, saying the same word several times until Billy finally understood – she was trying to say 'boat' in English, her accent making it sound Polish.

Billy let himself be pulled along, nodding at George to follow. Anya's mother pushed into the crowd, carrying Anya and holding Billy's hand, and still managing to shepherd her other daughters along in front of her.

'Hey, who do you think you're shoving, Mrs?' said a tetchy voice. A young man had turned to glare at them. His hair was parted in the middle, a thin moustache clung to his top lip, and he wore a sharp suit. But his face was pale and frightened.

'Back off there, let the women and kiddies through!' somebody yelled.

'It's not *just* women and kiddies, is it?' said the young man, his tone even more petulant.

But no one was listening to him, and the crowd parted, allowing Anya's mother up to the handrail with her children and Billy and George.

A little further along a section of the handrail was open and a seaman was helping passengers into a lifeboat, the last one on this side of the ship as far as Billy could see. The crowd watched sullenly, and Billy soon realised why. The people getting into the lifeboat were clearly first-class passengers, and those making up the crowd clearly weren't. Three burly seamen held them back.

Behind them stood someone Billy recognised. Mr Ismay was obviously in charge, deciding who was allowed in the lifeboat and who wasn't.

'First class only in this boat, I'm afraid,' said one seaman. He held up a hand, but Anya's mother knocked it aside and unleashed a torrent of Polish at him.

'Shame on you!' somebody yelled. 'Let the kiddies on the lifeboat!'

'There's no more room, I tell you, no room,' the seaman shouted back.

'You're lying!' somebody screamed. 'There's space on the benches!'

Billy looked over the handrail and saw that most of the benches were full. The first-class passengers sitting on them – women and children for the most part, and a few men as well – looked embarrassed and even ashamed. But there was a small space on one bench, a space just big enough for Anya and her mother and sisters.

Billy looked at Mr Ismay and his heart hardened against him.

'Mr Ismay,' he called out.

Mr Ismay looked up.

'Everyone can see there's room enough in the boat for these wee girls and their ma,' said Billy loudly. 'Or are you just going to let them drown along with the rest of us poor people? Maybe the other fine folk in this boat will tell all their fancy friends about it when you get to New York.'

Billy pushed Anya's mother and the girls up against the seamen. He stared hard at Mr Ismay, refusing to let him look away.

At last Mr Ismay nodded. 'Let them on,' he said quietly, and the seamen did as they were ordered, hurrying Anya and her family aboard. Anya's mother glanced back at Billy, but then she and the girls were gone and the seamen closed ranks again. Somebody yelled at them, and soon there was a scuffle. Billy retreated, looking for George.

He found him by the handrail further along the deck. The two boys looked down at the lifeboat as it was lowered to the sea. Anya was sitting on her mother's lap, looking up at them. Billy waved, and the little girl waved back.

'A long and happy life to you, Anya,' he said softly.

Chapter Twelve

Last Moments

'What now, Fleming?' said George, turning to Billy. 'You're the man with the answers. Although I don't think we'll be getting on any lifeboats in the near future. I'm pretty sure they've all been launched, full or not.'

'You're not wrong there,' said Billy.

He didn't have any more answers. He felt bruised and exhausted and frozen to his bones, and part of him wanted to lie down and die, to wait for the dark sea to swallow him. But he couldn't say that, not with George staring at him so hopefully.

'We should try to find Mr McElroy,' Billy said. 'If anyone knows what to do, he will.'

It seemed to make sense to head for the bellboy station, even though that meant going towards the submerged section of the ship.

The decks were still full of people, but none took any notice of the boys. Most were searching for lifejackets, and Billy saw several fights over these precious objects. He saw people leaping from the handrail and into the sea, which didn't seem a good idea.

Further on a priest with a powerful voice led others in a hymn Billy recognised.

Eternal Father, strong to save,
Whose arm hath bound the restless wave,
Who bidd'st the mighty ocean deep
Its own appointed limits keep;
Oh hear us when we cry to Thee,
For those in peril on the sea.

They found the Chief Purser in his office. He was calmly emptying his desk drawers and putting papers in his pockets. He looked up and frowned.

'Where have you two been?' he said. 'I put the rest of the bellboys into a lifeboat half an hour ago. You might well have missed your chance now. And what happened to your uniforms? You look like a couple of scarecrows!'

'Sorry, sir,' said Billy. 'I... I mean we... we were helping passengers...'

'Don't be daft, you've no need to apologise,' said George, rounding on him. 'He wasn't just helping passengers, Mr McElroy. He saved my life and the life of a little girl, so he did. And he got her and her family into a lifeboat.'

'Is that right?' said Mr McElroy. He came out from behind his desk and put a hand on Billy's shoulder. 'I knew you were a good lad from the moment I set eyes on you. Can I assume you boys have also settled your differences?'

'Aye, that you can, sir,' said George. He turned to Billy once more and held out his hand. 'You've got more guts than I'll ever have. You offered me your friendship once and I didn't take it. I hope you'll forgive me, Billy.'

Billy smiled and took his hand. 'There's nothing to forgive, George.'

'Right, come on, lads,' said Mr McElroy. 'We might still be able to help some of the passengers. And we should find out what's happening in the Marconi Room. I think Mr Phillips and Mr Bride are still in there.'

'Don't worry, sir, I'll check on them,' said Billy. 'I'll be right back.'

Mr McElroy was right. Mr Phillips and Harold were in the Marconi Room, tapping away at their Morse keys, even though the cabin was now leaning at a crazy angle.

'Good to see you, Billy,' said Harold. 'We're about to pack it in.'

'Did you hear from any ships?' said Billy. 'Are there any near?'

'Yes, there's one, the Carpathia,' said Harold. 'It's on its way.'

'It will be at least four hours before they get here,' said Mr Phillips. 'We'll be long dead by then, you mark my words. A watery grave is a terrible thing...'

'Hark to old misery here!' said Harold. 'While there's life, there's hope, that's what my dear old Ma always used to say. Come on, Jack, leave it.'

He dragged Mr Phillips away from the desk and thrust a lifejacket at him.

'I've a spare one for you, Billy,' Harold added. 'Here, put this on, and make sure you do it up.'

Billy did as he was told, and the three of them left the Marconi Room. The panic was worse than ever, the ship sinking ever further under the cold sea, its insides groaning ever more loudly.

'Hang on, what are they up to?' said Harold, pointing at a group of men on the bridge. They were wrestling with something, a long wooden shape – and as Billy looked he saw that it was a boat.

He ran off to tell Mr McElroy and George.

'Of course, the collapsible lifeboats!' said Mr McElroy. 'I saw two being launched so I assumed they'd all gone already. But there are another two stored on the roof of the bridge...'

Moments later they climbed the ladder that led to the roof of the bridge. It leaned down at a steep angle and one edge was below the water. Harold and Mr Phillips were there, along with a dozen men – a couple of officers, deckhands, even some passengers. They were all working on the two remaining boats, raising their canvas sides and knocking into place the ribs that would stiffen them.

Suddenly the roof of the bridge juddered and a huge wave surged across it, sweeping away one of the boats and the men working on it.

'Don't let the other one go!' yelled an officer, and they tried to hold on to it, Billy and George leaping forward to grab the wooden gunwale. The ship seemed to judder again, the roof dipping further below the water, and the second boat was swept away too, tipping over as it hit something – and dragging Billy into the sea with it.

There was no great splash. One minute Billy was on the roof of the bridge and the next he was in the water, completely disorientated. He kicked and thrashed and the sea roared in his ears, and just when he thought his lungs were about to burst he shot into the air and bobbed on the surface. The lifejacket had saved him.

But where was everybody? And where were the two boats?

He coughed and spat out seawater and tried to focus, but his eyes stung and for a while he couldn't see anything at all. He could hear the shouts and screams of people in the water around him. He shouted too, calling 'George!' and 'Mr McElroy!' over and over again, but there were no replies. Then he heard a terrible grinding noise and looked round just as his eyes cleared.

He found himself looking at the stricken Titanic. The wave that had swept him off the roof of the bridge must have been a big one, for he was at least a hundred yards from the ship. Its lights still glowed, but it was tilted steeply downwards, its gigantic stern now a couple of hundred feet above the water.

Suddenly a great crack appeared round the base of the leading funnel. It tipped over, smashed into the superstructure, then hit the sea with a colossal splash.

There were screams from the ship and the sea, and more when the second funnel followed the first. Billy floated, horrified and fascinated by what he was seeing. It was like being in the front row of a theatre watching the most amazing spectacle in the world, the last moments of a great ship. It was tilted so steeply now he thought the end must be soon. But there were more surprises to come.

The grinding noise grew louder as the ship's stern rose further from the water. The lights went out at last with a great fizzing, and there were other sounds as well, crashes and bangs and booms, and Billy had a sudden vision of what must be happening inside that enormous, hollow structure. Everything that wasn't bolted down or riveted in was falling towards the bow – furniture and trunks and chests and crockery and tools and people. Judging by the volume of sound even things that were bolted down were falling as well now.

Then huge cracks appeared in the side of the hull about a third of the way back from the bow. The cracks grew wider until the hull finally split in two, the whole forward section of the ship shearing off and going under the frothing sea in a cloud of steam and smoke.

The rest of the ship fell back onto its bottom, the last two funnels falling off, one on either side, and Billy could see the tiny figures of people dropping from the handrail or clinging on for dear life.

They didn't have long to wait. The ship's stern began to tip up once more and within seconds it was almost standing in the water.

Billy heard terrified screaming and watched as the tiny, ant-like figures scrambled upwards, away from the relentless water. Many of them jumped or fell as the last part of the Titanic sank down and vanished entirely in a final, terrible maelstrom.

Billy could still hear people calling out and thrashing in the water around him, but the noises soon faded. The sea was draining the warmth from him, and he felt as if his blood was turning into ice, sharp crystals crackling through his veins. He couldn't feel his feet or his legs any more, and he shivered, his whole body juddering. Then the ice reached his chest and the shivering stopped. It was strange, but the cold had penetrated so deeply that he almost felt warm again.

Billy was filled with a strange calmness. He leaned back, spread his arms in the water and looked up. There were so many stars, a host of lights sprinkled across the blackness. He thought of everything he'd seen, images from the last few crazy hours spinning through his mind. He thought of Ma and his sisters. He thought of Da, and wondered if he might be seeing him again soon, and whether Da had been watching when he had saved Anya. Billy hoped so.

He closed his eyes and let the water cover his mouth.

He didn't hear the lifeboat approaching, or feel the hands that roughly hauled him from the sea.

Chapter Thirteen

The Lucky Ones

Billy didn't remember much of what happened over the next few hours. He woke up to find himself being carried onto another ship, and wondered briefly how somebody had managed to re-float the Titanic so quickly. But it wasn't the Titanic, it was the ship Harold had spoken of, the RMS Carpathia.

Three days later Billy was at the Carpathia's handrail as it steamed past the Statue of Liberty and into New York harbour. By then he had discovered just how lucky he had been. Most of the lifeboats had got as far away from the Titanic as possible, their occupants afraid of being sucked down by the sinking ship or swamped by the people in the water. Billy had been saved because he had been alone and the lifeboat had almost run him down.

A huge crowd clamoured on the pier as the Carpathia docked – people desperate for news of their families, reporters yelling questions, the New York police trying to hold them back.

To his relief, Billy was whisked off with the other survivors to a hostel. There he was given a complete change of clothes – he was still wearing the trousers and pullover he had found in the abandoned cabin with George and Anya. Then he curled up on a bunk and slept for two days.

A week later, a man from the White Star Line's Manhattan office came to see him. Most of the American survivors had gone home by now, but plenty of people from other countries had been on the Titanic and they were still waiting until they were well enough to go on to their final destinations. Others – especially those who had lost loved ones – simply wanted to go home, and were waiting for their passages to be arranged. By now Billy knew there had been over 2,200 people on the ship, and over 1,500 of them had died. So he really had been one of the lucky ones.

The man from the White Star Line wrote down Billy's name in a notebook, and told him the company would pay for his passage home to Belfast.

'Can I ask you something?' said Billy. 'Is there a list of survivors?'

'Sure is,' said the man, smiling. He was plump and balding and had a strong New York accent. 'I got a copy of it right here with me. Who are you looking for? Captain Smith isn't on it, and neither is Mr Andrews. They went down with the ship, which seems right, I reckon, as one of them was the captain and the other one built it. Maybe Mr Ismay should have done the same.'

Billy had read some of the New York newspapers, so he knew that Mr Ismay wasn't the most popular man in the world at the moment. It seemed that he had escaped in one of the collapsible lifeboats before the end, and the newspapers had said quite openly he was a coward who should have given his place to somebody more deserving. Many women and children had died. Most of them had been third-class passengers.

'What about the officers?' said Billy. 'Did Mr McElroy make it?'

The man frowned and ran his eyes down the list. After a while he looked up and sadly shook his head. 'Sorry,' he said. 'Was there anybody else?'

'Anderson,' Billy said. 'George Anderson.' The man ran his eyes down the list again, and once more shook his head.

Poor George, Billy thought, closing his eyes to remember his friend. That only left Anya and her mother and sisters.

'What about a little Polish girl called Anya?' he said. 'Is she on the list?'

The man ran his eyes down the list one more time and Billy held his breath. At last the man looked up at him with a smile.

'Well, I don't think I can say her last name – it's full of c's and z's,' he said, pronouncing the last letter as 'zee' in the American way. 'But there's definitely an Anya, and there are four others with the same surname – they're listed here as a mother and four daughters.'

At last, Billy smiled too. He found out later that Anya and her mother and sisters had been sent to Ellis Island, the place where immigrants to the USA were processed. As survivors of the sinking of the Titanic they would definitely be allowed to stay. It was strange to think that a boy from Belfast had saved a little girl from Poland he had only met days before. Strange, but good.

* * *

Two weeks later Billy was on a small steamer heading back across the Atlantic along with the small number of White Star Line employees who had survived. To his surprise he didn't feel at all scared. If anything, he felt at home on a ship, pleased to feel the deck throbbing beneath his feet and know that he still had his sea legs while others didn't.

There was one moment of sadness. The ship stopped in mid-ocean to lay a wreath at the spot where the Titanic had gone down. A vicar led the ship's company and passengers in prayer and they sang hymns, their voices whipped away by the wind. It was a blustery day, the sky full of grey clouds, and Billy looked down at the wreath floating forlornly on the green waves. But he didn't cry.

Eventually they arrived in Belfast. Billy stood at the handrail, staring at the red-brick terraces and the Harland and Wolff gantries and the graveyard where his Da was buried. He could hardly believe that none of it had changed.

His street hadn't changed either, and neither had his old front door. He rapped on it as if he were a stranger, and it was a while before it opened. Little Mabel stood in the hallway looking up at him with a frown. Then she turned round and ran back down the hall, yelling. 'Ma! Our Billy is home!'

Billy laughed. It was grand to be back, so it was.

Postscript

A Titanic Story

I have to confess that I was never very interested in the story of the Titanic. I knew about the sinking, of course. I remember seeing the 1958 film when I was very young and thinking how terrible it all was, but it didn't have that much impact on me. I was very taken with James Cameron's epic version of the story. When *Titanic* came out in 1997 I went to see it twice, but it was still just a movie.

Then my son Tom and I were asked to write this book, and we both started to read about the great ship and that terrible night in April 1912, and soon I began to realise how the story of what happened can draw you in.

There's something about it that exerts a powerful influence. Maybe it's the fact that the disaster was a result of a number of small mistakes that added up to a catastrophe. Maybe it's the inevitability of it all once the iceberg had been struck. Maybe it's to do with discovering that the big story is made up of all the smaller stories of everyone on the ship – although for each person it was a very big event indeed.

Billy and his family are fictional creations, but it's true that building the Titanic was a big achievement for the Harland and Wolff shipyard, a business the people of the city were proud of. Boys became apprentices at fourteen, and working in the shipyard was hard. Eight men died while the Titanic was being built. George is also fictional, though the job of bellboy is real.

The rest of the ship's crew named in the story are real people. Captain Smith and Officers Wilde, Murdoch and Moody all died, and their bodies were never recovered. The same is true of Chief Purser McElroy. You can find pictures on the internet of Titanic's officers, and Mr McElroy is in the back row. We thought he had a friendly face, so in our story he became a friend to Billy and George.

Mr Andrews is known to have worked hard getting people into lifeboats or provided with lifejackets. He was last seen alone in one of the lounges, and went down with the ship he had designed. His body was never found either.

Mr Lightoller survived, and on BBC iPlayer you can even hear an interview with him about the sinking, recorded in the 1930s. (*bbc.co.uk/archive/titanic/5047.shtml*)

Jack Phillips and Harold Bride both stayed in the Marconi Room sending distress signals until the last minute, and both were there when the last collapsible lifeboats were swept into the sea. Jack Phillips managed to get on board one, but died of exposure while they were waiting to be rescued. Harold Bride was swept into the sea, but managed to get into the boat and lived.

Mr Ismay survived, and was heavily criticised for doing so. The accounts differ, and some people said in his defence that he helped many women – third-class passengers as well as first-class – into lifeboats, before finally taking a place in one of the collapsibles only when there was nobody else to give it to.

Anya and her family are fictional, but they're typical of Titanic's third-class passengers. If they had been real, they would have been among the luckiest people on the Titanic that night, because only a quarter of all the third-class passengers survived. All of the first- and second-class children on board were saved – but only one-third of the third-class children found a place in a lifeboat. And while almost all the women in first class survived, fewer than half of the women in third class did.

Men in all classes died in great numbers, because of the 'women and children first' policy. Only a third of first-class male passengers survived – but those with the worst chance by far were second- and third-class male passengers. Most of them died.

It's not clear why the death rate was so heavily linked to how much you paid for your ticket. One factor was that the third-class cabins were at the bottom of the ship, and the first- and second-class passengers were nearer the lifeboats. Some reports say that third-class passengers were accidentally locked below decks. It's not clear if third-class passengers were deliberately held back by sailors. However, many people at the time believed that first-class passengers were given priority unfairly and others were turned away. We've taken this line in the story. The full truth may never be known.

Plenty of first-class male passengers didn't even try to get places in the lifeboats. The enormously wealthy Ben Guggenheim chose to go down with the ship. He sent a parting message to his wife saying, 'No woman shall be left aboard this ship because Ben Guggenheim is a coward.'

Out of 2,223 people on board when it hit the iceberg, 1,517 died.

Of course there are many books and websites and films about the Titanic. We hope you enjoy our re-imagining of this terrible event. For, however many times it's told, it was and always will be a titanic story.

Tom and Tony Bradman

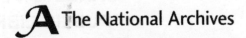